IT'S NOT ME, IT'S YOU

It's Not Me, It's You

Brian Kirk

SOUTHWORDeditions

First published in 2019
by Southword Editions
The Munster Literature Centre
Frank O'Connor House, 84 Douglas Street
Cork, Ireland

Set in Adobe Caslon 12pt

ISBN 978-1-905002-67-2

Contents

Acknowledgements

I'm grateful to the editors of the various magazines and journals who have published my stories over the years. "That New Girl" was published by *Willesden Herald New Short Stories* in November 2018; "The Shawl" was published in *The Long Story, Short* in March 2013; "The Invitation" was published in Issue 7 of *The Lonely Crowd* in June 2017. I'd like to acknowledge the support I've received from South Dublin County Council Arts Office by way of a bursary in 2017. I'd particularly like to thank John Murphy and Dermot Bolger who have acted as readers and mentors of my work over the years with unstinting honesty and unfailing support.

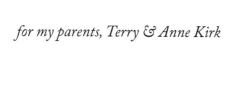

for my parents, Terry & Anne Kirk

THAT NEW GIRL

I was out on the balcony having a smoke with Daniel when the new girl was brought into Alastair's office. I had my back to the rail and was looking directly at Dan; he was telling me about some friend of his who'd mistakenly thought he'd developed a foolproof way of beating the house at blackjack. I wasn't really listening. I could see the new girl clearly as Sara led her through the open plan to the Chief Executive's office. The building is mostly glass and steel and you can see where everyone is at any given moment. For some reason I didn't point her out to Dan, even though a new girl always warranted attention from the guys. Perhaps I've matured since getting married. Or I like to think I have.

Later that afternoon Sara brought her around the floor making introductions. It's always pointless; the odds are against us in these cases. We all remember her name, but our names melt into the ether and she's compelled to admit over the ensuing days that she didn't manage to catch them. But there's always one guy she remembers straight away, and all across the floor looks are exchanged, eyebrows are raised. Everyone can see what's happening here.

By the way, it's never me. It's Dan, of course. He has that geeky hipster look that girls seem to go for these days. His hair is cut short at the back and sides, but his dark fringe falls across one side of his bearded face when he looks down. Within a day or two it's like she's been with the company for years. She's been out to lunch with Sara and the girls from Legal and she's calling Daniel 'Dan' like she's known him forever. She seems to spend an awful lot of time standing by his workstation on her way to and from the break-out area, a cup of coffee in one hand, the other resting lightly on a file balanced on the side of his desk. Dan winks at me when I pass behind her on my way to the photocopier. I pull a face, but I'm not sure what it's supposed to signify.

She doesn't say much to me. I'm not complaining or anything. I'm a couple of years older than Dan and I'm married so I must seem ancient to a girl like her who's fresh out of college. I remember before me and Sara got married some of the older guys on the floor saying how getting hitched had suddenly made them more attractive to women. My experience has been otherwise. That's not to say I'm looking to pick up girls these days. I'm not; I'm very happy with the life I have with Sara. I shouldn't be surprised that they'd lie about something like this because they lie about most things, I find: golf handicaps, the quality of hotels they stay in, but particularly they lie about girls. Anyway, when I was single I was never that popular with the girls, so I can't see how my being suddenly unavailable would affect anything either way. Sure, I enjoy a night out and used to do my best with the chat up lines when I had a few drinks inside me, but I was never a player; not the way Dan is. All the clichés you hear about women liking a bastard appear to be true in his case. For some reason this bothers me; probably because I consider myself a nice guy. Over the years that he's been with the company Dan's dated most of his female co-workers. Some have been one-night stands, some longer, but never for more than a month or two. I don't mean to judge him or anything, but somehow it doesn't seem right.

It's always the new girls he goes for. Fresh meat, he calls them. We laugh, Sara and I, when we talk about this. Sometimes I wonder if I behaved the way Dan does would people indulge me the way they indulge him. But that could never happen. There's something about him that makes people – both women and men – give him the benefit of the doubt; something that I don't possess.

On Friday we went out for drinks after work. We do this once a month or so; Alastair, the Chief Executive, encourages it from a team building point of view, putting cash behind the bar for food and drinks. We usually have pizza and beer, and then maybe more drinks or, if we're really up for it, we might go to a club after that. It always starts very sedately, people chatting and gossiping happily while they sip bottled beer and tear pizza slices out of boxes.

10

Later we fall into groups – gender-based usually – where the men discuss football and golf for a while before the subject inevitably turns to women. I don't mind; I'm not a prude. Sara is with the girls and I know they do something similar in their group, the conversation inevitably becoming less guarded as the wine flows.

As each hour passes we lose more and more from our groups until only the hard core are left and the sexes come together then to drink cocktails or shots. At this stage there are very few boundaries left. Everything that needs to be said can be said. Chances are no one will remember the next day anyhow.

It's just kicks, drinks and jokes, and maybe some karaoke if it really gets out of hand and we end up in that kind of place. Usually Sara and I give in by mutual choice before it descends too far and jump in a taxi. At home we make coffee and get ready for bed without saying much. The next morning our heads hurt but we put on a brave face. We sleep late and have brunch in front of the TV, the weekend supplements shared between us on the sofa.

I could have kept my mouth shut and let Saturday just happen as usual; the trip to the supermarket, the walk in the park later, but I found it impossible.

'So, what was she like?' I asked, as we prepared dinner later that evening.

'What was who like?'

'That new girl.' I stole a glance at Sara, but she was distracted, looking for something in a high cupboard. She didn't reply.

'Well?' I persisted.

'Have you seen the soy sauce?' She sounded annoyed.

I reached in behind her and put my hand on the bottle immediately.

'Well, what's she like then?' I asked again.

She ignored me as she tipped soy sauce into a clean bowl. I turned and stood like a fool with my hands by my sides looking out the front window where I could see the tops of some trees across the street. Our apartment is on the third floor and, even though we've been here for over a year, I'm still not used to living above ground level.

Eventually Sara finished juicing a lime and mixing it into the sauce. She turned to me then.

'Now, what's so urgent?'

'Nothing,' I said. 'I was just wondering what you thought of that new girl.'

'Not you as well!'

'What do mean, me as well?'

'Oh, you're all the same. Every time a new girl arrives you boys all go around with your tongues hanging out.'

'That's not fair!' I was hurt and wanted Sara to know it.

'Ah, come on, Mike. I'm just having some fun with you. But you know it's true. The way you guys go on.'

'Not me, though.'

'No, not you, pet.'

She leaned over and kissed me on the lips lightly. 'You're all mine, and you wouldn't dare look at any new girl!'

She laughed as she opened the fridge and took out a bowl of beef strips covered in cellophane.

I went to the bedroom and sat on the bed and read for a while. Or pretended to, at any rate.

When I came back to the kitchen the air was filled with steam and smoke and the sharp smells of spice and stir-fry. Sara looked up at me and smiled.

'Were you leaving me to do all the work? Come on, set the table for us now. It won't be long.'

I took two wine glasses off the shelf and some cutlery from the drawer, placed the salt and pepper pots carefully in the middle of our small round dining table. I rummaged in the drawer again and found the corkscrew and went at a bottle of red wine with it until it gave in with a satisfying pop. I poured a little into a glass and took a sip. The inside of my mouth felt like sandpaper, so I fetched two tall glasses from the high cupboard and filled them with cold water from the filter jug in the fridge.

'But seriously,' I said, 'what do you think of her?'

'She's alright.' Sara drained the noodles as she spoke. 'She's very keen on Dan.'

'I got that,' I said. 'Why is that?'

Sara laughed.

'Why are you so surprised? And why do you care? It's always the same with a new girl.'

Sara brought the plates over and I poured out two glasses of wine.

'He's charming, and good-looking too – it's no wonder the new girls are flattered by his attention,' she went on.

'Was it the same with you?' I asked. And immediately I regretted it.

Sara's face hardened. She didn't speak again for the duration of dinner. I didn't either.

For weeks Dan and the new girl were inseparable. When I'd step out on the balcony in the afternoon for a cigarette they'd exchange coy looks and nod to me, but each time they soon stubbed out their cigarettes and left me on my own.

When I complained to Sara she shook her head and laughed.

'Are you jealous?' she asked.

'Don't be stupid,' I said.

'I'm serious,' she said. Then she turned to me, smiling. 'I'm just not sure whether you're jealous of him or of her.'

'You're hilarious,' I said, forcing a smile, wishing I'd never said anything.

When I finally got a chance to talk to Dan he wasn't his usual forthcoming self.

'Yeah, she's cool,' was all he said.

'But, yeah, like… how?' I asked.

'A gentleman never tells, Mike. You should understand that.'

'If I ever meet a gentleman I'll bear it in mind,' I said.

He didn't react.

'So, you two are getting serious,' I said. It wasn't a question; it was me commenting on his life, something which he would normally intensely dislike. But he wouldn't be drawn.

'If I may quote another bearded, charismatic man from the dim and distant past: "it is you who say it".'

'What the hell is that supposed to mean?' I asked.

'What it says. I always loved that line,' he said. 'When faced with the accusation, "Are you the King of the Jews?" he comes back with that!' Dan says it again slowly, nodding: 'it is you who say it.'

'So now you're comparing yourself to Jesus Christ?'

'It is you who say it,' he said for the third time, smiling at me.

By the following Friday it was all off. I couldn't believe it. It became apparent at work that there was a problem; she didn't pause when she passed Dan's workstation and at smoke time he walked straight past her and signalled to me to join him on the balcony.

'Trouble in paradise?' I ventured when we'd both lit up.

He exhaled a long plume of smoke and sighed.

'I don't understand women,' he said, shaking his head. 'She knew it wasn't serious.'

'So, you finished with her?' I asked.

'It just came to a natural end really.'

'But she didn't see it that way.' Again, it wasn't a question. I stubbed out my cigarette and went back to my desk.

Later that afternoon the new girl asked for my help. She was having some trouble opening an application on her desktop and there was nobody else around. It was easy to sort out and I was happy to help. She brought me a coffee to say thanks and hung around my workstation for a while chatting. I could see Dan peering over his partition, probably wondering what she was doing with me. She was nice. Smart, but not overly confident; forward, but not so much to be thought of as pushy. She had blonde hair that fell to her shoulders, framing a clear-skinned face that held big blue eyes and a wide, red lipsticked mouth which broadened further when she smiled revealing even, white, American teeth.

'So how are you settling in?' I asked.

'Pretty good. The work is interesting,' she smiled.

'And the people?' I probed.

'You know…'

I didn't, so I asked again. 'Everyone treating you well?' I felt I had a right to ask, because of my age, my seniority on the floor.

She looked a little uncomfortable. She shook her head quickly.

14

'No, no, everyone's just great,' she said.

I noted the mixed messages; her negative body language versus her positive words. I knew the score. I smiled.

'If you ever need anything you know where I am,' I said. And I meant it.

We were having a smoke out on the balcony, as we had done most days during the week.

'I wouldn't ask, only I know you're a friend,' she said.

Dan was away for a few days and was not due back in work until the following Monday. She still talked about him from time to time – much to my annoyance – but not as much as before, and anyway I was happy enough just to be in her company.

'It's no problem,' I said.

'Are you sure?'

I could see Sara passing by my workstation on her way to Alastair's office. I noticed how she didn't look up to see if I was out on the balcony as she passed.

'Honestly, it's not a problem.'

'But I feel bad for asking. Maybe Sara has plans for you on Saturday morning,' she said.

Why would she mention Sara? This was worse than her going on about Dan all the time.

'Listen,' I said, 'it's just to move a few boxes and stuff on a Saturday morning. It won't take more than an hour or so, so don't worry. Okay?'

She stood up and stubbed out the remains of her cigarette. I stood up too. I felt like we were in a glass case – which we were in a way. Her hand brushed my arm; it was simply a gesture of thanks, signifying our new closeness I thought. But I was dismayed that I found myself anxiously scanning the floor for Sara.

Later I scolded myself for feeling guilty. We were just friends sharing a smoke break at work. But that night at home Sara seemed much quieter than usual.

On Friday night we went out again, but this time things were different. The usual staff groupings did not assemble on gender lines; instead the sexes chatted together in three or four mixed groups.

I wasn't sure how this had happened. I wondered was it somehow because Dan wasn't there, but no one else seemed to notice or care. People moved between groups freely, chatting and sharing jokes, and I remember thinking that Alastair would be pleased; that the atmosphere was truly one of a team working in harmony. I looked around and saw Sara deep in conversation with two guys from marketing who wouldn't normally have been close to her, and as I did I noticed the new girl beside me, smiling, looking straight into my eyes. We were in a large group, but as we talked we moved away a little and stood by the bar together.

'I hope you'll be okay to drive tomorrow,' she said.

I held up my beer bottle. 'I'll be fine once I stay on this stuff,' I said. 'It's the shots that do the damage.'

She looked younger than ever, her face flushed from the wine she was drinking or the heat of the packed pub. She seemed vulnerable. I wanted to put my hand on her bare forearm – not in a creepy way – but to reassure her that I was looking out for her, that I understood the insecurity of her position in the company and I was offering support. But I resisted the temptation.

We didn't talk much but the extended silences we shared as we stood at the bar together were not uncomfortable. Eventually some of the others pushed in beside us to order more drinks at the bar and our moment together was over.

People left one by one until there were maybe four or five of us left. Someone ordered tequila and then Sara was at my side. She smiled at me.

'You okay?' she asked, and she took my hand and squeezed it.

I nodded.

'Fine,' I said.

'I think it's time we left,' she said.

I looked across at the new girl as she took a shot glass from the counter and knocked it back. Her eyes glazed momentarily and then refocussed. She was looking straight at me.

'Have a shot, Mike,' she said, reaching over and taking my arm. For a moment I was held between the grips of two women and I didn't resist either one.

'We're going now,' Sara announced to the small group that remained. The new girl let go her grip, which was not very firm to begin with, and we found our coats and went out on the street. I felt light-headed in the cold air.

The next morning my head ached when the alarm sounded.

'Jesus, Mike, why did you set an alarm? It's Saturday for Christ sake!' Sara rolled over in the bed and pulled the duvet over her head.

I pulled back the covers and stood up unsteadily before making my way to the bathroom. I tried to be as quiet as possible, but when I sneaked back into the room to get my clothes I was surprised to find Sara sitting up in bed wide awake.

'Where the hell are you going at this hour?' she asked.

'I'm just running an errand,' I said. 'You go back to sleep. I'll be back before you get up.'

I found a pair of jeans and an old sweatshirt and pulled on some trainers.

'An errand,' she said. It wasn't a question, so I didn't reply.

'I'll be back in no time at all,' I said.

'It's her, isn't it?' she said then.

'Sorry?'

'You should be! You were all over her last night. It was embarrassing.'

'I'm just doing her a favour. She has some boxes to move to her new flat, but she has no one to help her. Dan was supposed to do it weeks ago, but he never got around to it.'

'I saw the way you were looking at her last night. Don't think I didn't notice you both going off on your own during the night to have some time together. Do you have any respect for me at all?'

'I don't know what you mean. I hardly know the girl. I just offered to help her out. If it's a problem, I'll phone and say I can't do it.'

'Okay, you do that!'

'What?' I didn't expect that.

'Phone and say you can't do it. Go on. Tell her anything! Tell her your jealous wife doesn't want you to go! But just do it.'

I went into the kitchen and shut the door behind me before dialling her number. She answered on the first ring. She sounded bright, as if she'd been up for hours.

'I'm sorry,' I said, 'I can't do it today. Yeah, I know it's short notice, but the car won't start – I think it might be the battery.'

'That's okay, Mike,' she said. 'Don't worry. I feel bad for asking you anyway. I'll figure something out.'

'I'm sorry,' I said again foolishly.

'Hey, it's no big deal. Last night was fun though, wasn't it? You guys should have stayed. We went to that karaoke place and it was the best!'

I rang off, not sure what to do now, resenting the way Sara had forced my hand when I was only trying to do a girl an innocent favour. I boiled the kettle and waited for her to get up. After an hour she arrived in her dressing gown. She looked exhausted.

'I made coffee,' I said.

'Are you still here?' There was acid in her tone.

'Looks like it,' I said.

She poured herself a mug of coffee and put bread in the toaster.

'I can't believe you let her wrap you around her finger like that! You're no better than the rest of them in there – with their talk about girls! New girls! Fresh meat!'

'I'm not like them!' I said.

'You're all the bloody same! And her, she knows what she's doing alright!'

'She doesn't deserve this. I was only trying to help her out.' I tried to be as calm as possible.

The toast popped.

'Oh yeah,' Sara laughed softly without much humour, 'and if she let you kiss her, what then?'

'Jesus Christ, Sara!'

'Struck a nerve, have I? You've thought about it though, haven't you?'

'I'm not listening to this. I'm going out,' I said. I got up to leave.

'Going to see what's-her-name?' she asked.

'Her name is Megan,' I said. 'You know her name, you could at least call her by it.'

I walked straight out then, and I think Sara was surprised because she followed me out to the front door.

'Hold on, hold on,' she said. 'We both need to take a moment here. Don't go running off. I know nothing's really happened. We just need to let ourselves cool down.'

I shrugged her off and stepped outside, pulling the door behind me with a bang.

The car started first time and I remember being surprised even though I knew that the flat battery story was just a lie that I'd made up. I drove around aimlessly for a while, but I think I knew I was always going to go to Megan's. I wanted to help her as I'd promised and show her and Sara that a guy can offer to help a girl out like that from time to time as a friend without any strings attached.

When I turned on to her street I saw Dan's car immediately. I kept driving, even when I saw them standing on the pavement. I kept driving even as they tried to flag me down, and I kept on driving until I took the slip road for the motorway. I drove for hours even though I knew that all roads would lead home eventually. I wasn't upset exactly. I was confused. I wasn't sure about anything anymore; about Megan, Dan or Sara, but most of all I wasn't sure about myself.

THE SHAWL

They found the shawl on the back of a chair in a bar, forgotten or discarded by its owner. It was beautiful, golden, with many coloured threads woven into it. Robert saw it first and showed it to Helen. He imagined an elegant older woman with pale complexion and red lips wearing it, loosely thrown around her shoulders against the chill of a late summer evening. They were about to leave and, rather than hand it in to the barman as she would normally have done, Robert watched as Helen simply folded it neatly and placed it in her bag.

It was a Friday night, and this was the manner in which their working week routinely ended: a few drinks with their colleagues and friends in a crowded, fashionable bar under the arches near one of the main railway stations in the city. That evening they left a little earlier than usual, and walked home, rather than taking a taxi as they would normally have done. Their route took them away from the modern glass and steel buildings of the business district, through the older, Georgian, part of the city and out along the canal towards their bland but functional apartment block.

Helen took the shawl from her bag, and Robert pulled it tightly around her shoulders as they walked. They were in their late twenties and had been living together for two years. They were still young enough to be concerned only about the present, content to let the future emerge as it would.

That night they did not turn on the TV or make coffee or tea, or even open a bottle of wine, when they got in. They went straight to the bedroom and Robert softly tugged the shawl from Helen's body, spinning her gently onto the bed. He quickly undressed while she lay back watching him. When he was naked he started to undress her slowly, removing each garment methodically, not kissing or even touching her flesh yet. When she was completely naked he reached down to the floor and took up the shawl from where it lay. He coiled it like a rope and bound her two hands loosely to the wrought iron headboard.

Helen's eyes opened in surprise as he did this, but she did not attempt to stop him. He felt a rush of excitement, a throb like a dull ache at the back of his skull, and he noticed how she smiled as she lay back on the covers, apparently surrendering herself to the exquisite otherness of restraint. Robert wasn't sure why he had done it. There was something about the shawl, and the way Helen was attracted to it, that told him it was okay.

When he woke the next morning, the shawl was still draped on the headboard, snaked around the curves of the wrought iron, while Helen slept on beneath it. Robert went to the kitchen and made breakfast, taking it to her in the bedroom on a tray. He woke her gently with a kiss on the cheek and she smiled at him crookedly in the way that he loved. First thing in the morning she looked like a young girl, trapped in those furtive waking moments before the adult Helen emerged. He kissed her again and straightened her pillows. He fingered the smooth silk of the shawl above her head as he did so, marvelling at how it felt somehow warm and cold, wet and dry, simultaneously. Neither one mentioned the use they had put it to the night before.

Most weekdays Robert met James for a game of squash before work. James was due to be married that autumn to Helen's friend Sandra, and he confided in Robert a great deal. Robert was not really interested in James' plans, but he was always polite, offering what little advice he was able to honestly give when he could. Robert understood that James considered they had plenty in common because of Robert's long-term relationship with Helen who was his fiancé's closest friend. But he resisted James' attempts to pigeonhole him or speak on his behalf, particularly when there were others around; people like Maxwell and Harris, who they often had lunch or coffee with. Maxwell particularly enjoyed ribbing James about his forthcoming wedding, and Robert often wondered how James was stupid enough to continue sharing his plans with them.

'I just can't believe it, James – you're actually going through with this… this… wedding?' Maxwell asked one day, as they sat over lattes.

'It's going to be the best day of my life guys!'

'Did he just say what I think he said?' Maxwell looked from Harris to Robert in a theatrical manner. He shook his head. 'No, he couldn't have.'

James just laughed, as he always did. Robert was sure that James actually enjoyed the attention – Sandra was in grave danger of playing second fiddle when the big day finally came around.

'Look. It's simple, James. You know that thing? Eh? That special thing you like that Sandra does for you now and again, when you've been civil with her mother, or when she's had a few shots? Yeah? You know what I'm talking about?'

Robert watched James redden while Maxwell nodded, and Harris sniggered like a schoolboy.

'I know you know! Well that's all ancient history the day you take those vows my friend. *Comprendez?* Never again! *Sayonara*, so long, *arrividerci!*'

'You just don't understand?' James pleaded. 'Tell them, Robert.'

Robert looked at James and then at Maxwell and Harris.

'Yeah, tell us, Robert!' Maxwell urged. 'Don't tell me you're getting married too?'

Robert simply shook his head. 'Don't be stupid,' he said.

'Thank God for that! I thought the whole world was going crazy there for a minute. You see James, Robert knows what side his bread is buttered on, eh? Don't you?' He threw his arm loosely around Robert's shoulder, causing him to shift involuntarily in his seat. 'Doesn't want to lose his… er… privileges, isn't that right, Rob?'

'Yeah. Right. Whatever.'

'I know you're just taking the piss, Maxwell. But one day you'll meet a girl you want to spend the rest of your life with.'

Robert wished James would just shut up.

'James, I'm beginning to think this wedding of yours is just an elaborate smokescreen. I mean, that is just about the gayest thing I have ever heard a supposedly straight man say!'

Robert made his excuses and left.

One night later that week while Helen was in the bathroom getting ready for bed, Robert quickly looked through her drawers for the shawl. He was disappointed but told himself that it was too late for sex anyway, that they both had an early start the next morning. He undressed, putting on the shorts and t-shirt he normally slept in, and went to the laundry basket with his old clothes. When he lifted the lid he immediately saw the shawl, half-hidden beneath his shirt from the previous day. He extracted it and held it to his face, breathing in its foreign odour, now infused with the scent of his and Helen's stale bodily secretions.

When Helen returned from the bathroom he was naked on the bed, the shawl beside him.

'It's your turn tonight,' he said, and handed it to her.

He crossed his wrists and held them up against the headboard. He watched her take the shawl and coil it, just as he had done the other night, tying him loosely to the wrought ironwork. Then she undressed for him, slowly, without making eye contact. Robert never knew such intense anticipation. As she climbed onto him she reached and switched off the bedside light. When his eyes adjusted to the darkness, he could see the outline of her form moving above him in the stray moonlight that filtered through the gap in the curtains, and he could feel her weight on him and the gentle pull of the golden rope that bound his wrists and tied him to this pleasure.

Now every night when they went upstairs to bed Robert took the shawl from its place in the laundry basket and held it to his face for a moment, inhaling deeply, caressing his skin with it, before taking it to the bedroom. When Helen came out of the bathroom, he would already be naked, the shawl coiled in his hands like a luxurious rope and he would pin her to the bed quickly and tie her up. Sometimes he undressed her first, sometimes not, he was so eager to have her helpless. Only when she was fastened to the bars was he happy to take his time, to extend his and her pleasure for as long as he could stand it.

But after some weeks Robert began to grow dissatisfied with the new routine of their lovemaking. At his desk at work he fell to imagining other ways in which he might restrain Helen. Over lunch he continued to sit with James and Maxwell and Harris, but he hardly listened to their talk at all. The conversation usually ran from sex to football to golf and back to sex, but lately a serious element had intruded; occasional snippets of information filtered down to them about possible cutbacks and the uncertainty of the firm's future. Robert ignored it and them, bored now as much by his friends as by the work.

Helen's birthday was two weeks before James and Sandra were due to marry, and every year Robert tried to buy her something expensive but also meaningful. In the jeweller's shop he found himself looking at engagement rings but smiled and shook his head when the assistant asked if he needed any help. They had never seriously discussed it, but he believed there was a tacit understanding between them that one day they would marry.

The morning of her birthday was like every other work day morning. They barely had time to sip a mug of coffee or take a bite or two of toast before they left. After she rose he left a card and two wrapped boxes on her pillow. He had also reserved a table at an expensive restaurant for that evening. Helen opened the card quickly and kissed him on the lips. The presents would have to keep until later; there was no time to dawdle.

That night over dinner they talked about Sandra and James and the wedding.

'She's so excited, Rob – I don't think she can wait another two weeks.'

'Well, she's positively sober compared to James. He's ridiculous the way he goes on. You know what Maxwell is like; James just feeds him ammunition all day.'

'I think it's sweet, you know, the way he's as excited as Sandra. That's the way it should be. I mean, nobody's forcing them to get married, so they should be equally happy.'

'I know. It's just rare, I suppose, to come across a guy who actually displays his excitement about something like that.'

'Would you rather he pretended it was a chore?'

'No, no. It's not that. I'm sure almost all blokes who get married are happy about it, it's just that they don't go on about it the way James does.'

'It's a girl thing, you mean?'

'Kinda, I suppose.'

'That's a stereotype thing, Rob – kinda.' She grimaced. It was plain that she was cross.

'Ah, I know. I can't explain it. James is just over the top, that's all.'

He felt guilty, but also distracted by the prospect of the sex they would have later and continued to talk and smile at her although he could plainly see she was not impressed by what he'd said. He tried to maintain a pretence of celebration, but the good had gone out of the evening. He ate his food without appetite and sipped the expensive wine, but both were tasteless and did not fill him up. As they left he felt hollow, fragile, as though he might break if he fell over.

That night when they got home, they sat on the bed side by side while Helen opened her presents. The first was a bracelet, antique silver inset with delicate amber gemstones, expensive, one she had admired in a jeweller's shop window months before. She smiled and kissed him, and he tried to shake off the lethargy that had overtaken him in the restaurant, telling himself that he had bought her the present with his customary loving care. Nothing had changed; nothing was wrong. The second box was also luxuriously wrapped. It almost seemed wrong to tear the paper, but when Helen finally lifted the lid Robert saw over her shoulder an explosion of bright and dark colours, and for a moment he forgot what he had given her. It appeared to be a box of coloured lights. Then he watched her hand disappear inside and he remembered how it would feel cool and smooth like cream. Not lights, no, but scarves of many colours, made of Indian silk.

Then Robert was kissing her, lifting her up on to the bed. He used the shawl to tie her hands together to the headboard, before he started taking off her clothes. He slowly opened the buttons of her blouse, but he could not remove it completely because of the way she was restrained. He then pulled off her skirt and tights and pants, and when he had done this he took two of the silk scarves from the gift box and, spreading her legs wide, he fastened each of Helen's feet to the bottom bed posts. He looked at her, but she had turned her head away towards the door.

'Robert,' she said quietly, her face still averted.

'Sssh, love, don't say anything.'

He started to get undressed, standing some feet away from the bottom of the bed, greedily examining every inch of her helpless, naked body as he let his clothes fall one by one to the floor. Before he even touched her, he took the remaining scarf from the box and tied it firmly around her eyes, blocking out the light. Then he waited. He could hear his heart beat against the wall of his chest; he could feel the blood surge through his veins. He would have liked to remain there just watching her bound body spread out before him. The open bedroom window behind the drawn shade welcomed a cool breeze, and Robert could see goose bumps appearing on Helen's pale exposed flesh. Finally, he touched her, making her flinch, which only added to his excitement. He quickly pushed inside her and came with a stifled grunt within a few moments. He cursed silently and went to the bathroom to wash himself.

'Robert! Robert! Where are you?'

'It's okay, I'm here, I'm here.'

He undid her feet first and then her hands, and she lifted the scarf from her eyes while he stood with his back to her, swiftly pulling on his shorts and t-shirt. He caught sight of himself in the mirror and was startled to find that he did not look like himself, or as he thought himself to be, with his back rounded, hunched over, hurriedly dressing. Helen went to the bathroom to pee and when she returned moments later he was already under the covers with his back to her, his face to the wall, emitting the regular breaths of one who is sleeping. She climbed into bed beside him, switched off the side light, and lay down.

'Happy birthday, Helen,' he said, and he turned and kissed her softly on the forehead.

On the day of the wedding all the talk was about the restructuring. After all the elaborate plans they had made no one seemed to pay much attention to James and Sandra. The guests at each table in the dining room carried on hoarse, whispered conversations while the speeches droned on from the top table.

'What about Gordon? Is he gone too?'

'Yes, and Nicholls on the fifth floor, and that girl who works with them, Stephanie, I think her name is.'

'Jesus! That must be almost half the brokers and more.'

The Friday before an impromptu meeting had been called by the management in the afternoon and Robert had been among those who were let go. He was still in shock now, sitting beside Helen at a table full of ex-colleagues, listening to them talk about him as if he was not there, as if he was invisible. He could feel Helen's eyes on him, saw her concern in how she tried to ration his drinks. He had bottled beer in the bar earlier and wine with the meal, and now the waitresses were filling glasses with champagne for the toasts. It felt wrong, all this celebration and raising of glasses when his future was so uncertain.

'Try to enjoy the day, Rob. It's James and Sandra's day – don't spoil it. There are other jobs out there for you. You have contacts, you'll be okay,' Helen whispered to him, putting her hand on his. He left his hand where it was until she took her own away.

They retired to their room that night as soon as politeness allowed. The hotel was plush, the room large, the bed substantial. They undressed silently by the light from the open en suite bathroom door. Robert climbed hastily into bed while Helen searched in her overnight bag for her cleansing and moisturising creams. He pretended to sleep when she lay down beside him. Neither one moved. He listened to his own even breathing, dismayed by its tired regularity.

In the first few weeks Robert tried hard. He devoured the job vacancy pages of the newspapers each day and emailed the agencies regularly. He called all his contacts and tried to sound off-hand but confident when he spoke of his future. He kept the apartment clean and tidy, and he cooked dinner for Helen every evening when she came home. It soon became apparent that there were no jobs out there in his field; all of the other firms had downsized too. There were probably hundreds of replicas of him all over the city looking at the same papers and websites every day.

He no longer instigated sex at night; in fact, they only ever made love now when Helen took the lead, which was not often. He no longer looked for the shawl at bedtime and most nights retired long before her.

In idle moments he began to imagine an alternative life; perhaps he would do some travelling, experience new things. He had a friend in Berlin who had promised a place for him to stay if he ever wanted it. At night when he couldn't sleep, while he listened to Helen's shallow breathing, he imagined the new life he might enjoy there in the coffee shops and bars. But in his heart he knew that he would never do it.

He spent more and more time on the laptop during the day. He read news stories, sports reports and celebrity gossip, all without any great interest. He visited porn sites and idly scrolled through pages and pages of images of naked women. Some days he did not even get hard. The apartment became untidy; dust settled on the mantle and the window sills and the tops of cupboards in the kitchen. The sink was always full of unwashed dishes, the laundry basket full of unwashed clothes. Often when Helen came home he would be watching TV, so she would phone for pizza.

They argued all the time. About the dirt and the mess, and the fact that he had stopped looking for work, but Robert knew it was all about her really. She was changing, and it frightened him. He met James for lunch one day, for the first time since he was let go, hoping to find out something about what Helen was thinking through his friend's wife.

'Jesus you look like shit, Robert.'

'Thanks.'

They were having coffee in a cafe far away from the firm to ensure that Maxwell or Harris would not be around.

'No luck on the job front then?'

'No.'

'Are you looking?'

'Of course I'm looking! Do you think I want to hang around all day doing nothing?'

James laughed. 'Watching internet porn all day – that's what Maxwell says you're doing.'

'He's just jealous! How did he avoid the chop anyway?'

'Who knows! Hey, we should play squash some morning again. It's been ages.'

'My gym membership went with the job – remember?'

James looked embarrassed. 'Sorry. But you can be my guest.'

'Okay, we'll do it. So how is married life?'

'Robert, you have no idea. Best thing we ever did!'

'Maybe I should propose to Helen – what do you think?'

James laughed. 'Yeah, why not.'

So, Robert and James started playing squash again, and Robert phoned his contacts again and started reading the job vacancy columns and emailing the agencies. He began to cook meals every evening and he set about tidying the apartment. He found the shawl in a bag that Helen had packed for the charity shop hidden away in a closet. He took it out and held it to his face. Its distinctive smell was almost gone, but the feel of the silk on his fingers and face brought him back to months before, when he and Helen had been close. He clung to that. He hid it discreetly in a drawer in the bedroom beneath his socks and underwear.

That night when Helen came home there were candles on the table and red wine in large glasses. There was bread and olives on a plate, and the rustic smell of tomatoes and garlic filled the air. Helen looked tired. He tried to be attentive, but natural. He had showered and shaved and dressed smartly for a change. While she waited for her meal he smiled at her and made small talk.

'I made some calls today. There's a chance they might want someone over at Brown's by the end of the month. I'm just waiting on a call back.'

'That's great.'

In his heart he knew it was bullshit – Brown's weren't hiring, everyone knew that; in fact, they were almost at the wall.

He spent the whole evening following her around the small apartment, filling her glass, getting the paper, her book, changing the channel for her.

'I'm tired, I'm going to bed,' she said after a while. It was still very early.

He stayed on the sofa watching the TV while she went to the bathroom to scrub her make-up and the day's grime from her face.

When she emerged, Robert was lying on the bed, naked, the shawl twisted in his white-knuckled hands like a venomous snake.

'Lie down, Helen,' he said. 'It's been too long.'

He felt powerful again, aware of his lean, strong, hairless body under Helen's gaze. His genitals, half-aroused, moved into life.

'No, Rob,' she said. 'I'm tired.'

'But, Helen, the shawl,' he said, and he stood up and thrust it out to her as if it was a living thing, as if he was some kind of savage without words to explain his meaning, as if the shawl itself held all the meaning there could be.

'No, Robert. That's not going to happen. I'm not in the mood.'

He felt himself go flaccid now, and he continued to shrink as he stood there before her. His face reddened a little; it made him feel young, foolish, almost childish. She turned her back on him and began to get undressed, speaking calmly over her shoulder.

'I've been thinking anyway, Robert. I'm taking a break from work – I'm going away for a while. This thing with us, I think it's over. It's not going anywhere. You know I'm right. It's for the best if we just stop right now.'

He heard himself make a peculiar noise, more animal than human, but she ignored it or pretended not to hear. She must have known that he was crying. All he wanted was for her to look at him.

THE INVITATION

When the wedding invitation arrived I felt nothing at all, not even pleased for my old friend. I should have destroyed it and never mentioned it to Magda. When I showed it to her she said immediately that I must go. Of course, she would not be going; she was six months pregnant with our first child and anyway she had never met Pete, or any of my Dublin friends for that matter.

So, I agreed to go, reassured mainly because I would be on my own, that I would not have to introduce her to a past I'd spent years escaping from. As the day of my departure drew nearer I found myself thinking about the place more and more, remembering little bits and pieces of a life that was undoubtedly mine but which I now hardly recognised. I found Pete on Facebook – everyone in Ireland seems to be addicted to social media – but I didn't follow him. Instead I scrolled through hundreds of pictures of my old friends and watched them age ten years in minutes. I studied the face of his young bride-to-be also, some six years younger than him, and then I studied pictures of her friends; they seemed like kids, impossibly young and uniformly pretty.

If you've never been to Swords you haven't missed much. It's right beside the airport where the Northside becomes North County Dublin. It's both rural and urban, containing within it the worst elements of both; some tillage, but plenty of green grass and waste land dotted with burnt-out cars and piebald horses. The wider hinterland is a scattering of car hire businesses and industrial units with links to the airport. Even when I was growing up it suffered from a split personality as much as we, its denizens, did. Before they built the motorway you had to pass through Swords on your way from the city to Drogheda, Dundalk and ultimately Belfast, but now the town has spread like a tidal line of scum washed up between the sea and the M1. It is effectively one long wide main street (as so many Irish towns are) lined with shops, pubs, cafes and the like. At one end is a castle and at the other end is the school where Pete and I spent our teenage years. Both have been altered dramatically, and ostensibly for the better, since I left. These are the first things I notice as the taxi takes me into town.

When I check in to my room at the hotel that used to be a pub I sit on the bed and begin to dial Pete's number, but something stops me. It's early still, only three o'clock, and I fear that, once I call him, I will be tied to him for the whole weekend. He will invite me to his parents' house or he will want me to go for drinks in the afternoon. I can't decide which option appeals to me less.

I put the phone away, hang up my suit and lay my small case on the end of the bed. I am always acutely aware of my solitary self when I check into hotel rooms without Magda. I shower and dress slowly and prepare to leave. I'm not sure what I'm about to do, but I need to get out of the room; there is a sickly-sweet smell in the air and the drone of the extractor fans from the kitchen below is inducing a mild headache. I text Magda quickly: *Just in now. All good x.*

Out on the street the town seems much busier than I remember. I assumed with the motorway and all the new roads that by-pass the centre of town that the place would be quiet and forlorn, but far from it. It's Friday afternoon and the kids are just out of school and the supermarkets are full of shoppers, the pavements crowded with both. I pass a chip shop where we used to go for lunch from school on Fridays years before. I remember how we'd sit in a booth, four or five of us, talking and slagging each other, brutal yet sensitive, conscious of our own separateness in the way only teenagers can be, watching the convent girls as they passed by the plate glass windows. Marks out of ten we gave them. The same jokes every week, the same reactions, high fives and shoulder punches; more ritual than conversation.

'I thought it was you, Patrick!'

I feel a punch on my upper arm and look around to find a familiar face, but the name won't come straight away, so I smile at him.

'Pete will be made up to see you!'

'How are you keeping?' I ask. Kevin. His name is Kevin, but we called him Jeff for some reason.

'Kevin,' I say, taking his hand in mine. He pulls me towards him and gives me an awkward man-hug. I am surprised by that to say the least. We never used to do these physical displays of affection.

'How long has it been? Seven, eight years?'

'And the rest,' I say.

'Longer? Jayz! Well you haven't changed much. How is Germany then?'

'I'm in Denmark – Copenhagen actually.' Even to myself I sound like a little shit.

'Yeah right,' Kevin says, without showing any evidence of being annoyed with me. 'Have you seen Pete yet?'

'No, I've just arrived. I was just about to call him.' I take out my phone. I can see there is a message from Magda.

'Come on with me, I know where he is right about now.' Kevin looks at his watch and starts walking.

I follow him down the street past gangs of uniform-clad teenagers who jostle us and shout through us at each other as if we don't exist. I sneak a look at Magda's message as we go: *Have fun! Hugs from M and little T xx.* That's our thing: we call the foetus Teddy because he looks like a little bear on the twenty-week scan.

Pete looks just like his photos on Facebook. A little flabby around the cheeks, the eyes smaller and sunken, but his hair is still that sandy brown it always was. It's far too long also, and I wonder as he beams at me if he'll get it cut before the wedding. He stands to greet me and, just like Kevin, he throws his arms around me. It still feels wrong, as if they are making themselves do it for my benefit, but I go along with the hug anyway although I sense his body tensing as he approaches me.

I expected that it would be a pub, but instead Kevin has led me to a warehouse on the edge of town, past rows and rows of sofas and coffee tables and on out the back to a prefabricated building where Pete, dressed in old jeans and a Man United top, sits in a lazy-boy chair in front of a flat screen TV. When he sees me he drops the controller and pulls off his headphones.

'You came! You fucker!'

I nod. 'Well, you invited me, Pete.'

Then the hug thing.

'So how the bloody hell are you?'

'I'm good,' I say.

He looks at Kevin and then at me and then he speaks, more to Kevin than me.

'Can you believe it? Eh? God, he looks well though, doesn't he?'

I laugh. 'You're not doing too bad yourself,' I say.

He shakes his head, watching me all the time, reading my thoughts.

'You're probably wondering about all this.' He indicates the almost empty room, the TV, the games console on the floor, a small desk and chair in the corner with a laptop open on it. I say nothing.

'It's Amy – you know what women are like. We all need some space every now and again. Well, this is my space. We've been living in each other's pockets for months, and it's only going to get worse after tomorrow.' He laughs quickly, and this time Kevin laughs too. They sound identical, like they've been seeing too much of each other. 'This is work, Patrick, yeah? This is me working late, okay? You know about these things I'm sure. How long have you been hitched?'

'I'm not married,' I say.

'Ah come on now! You know what I mean – you and...'

'Magda,' I say.

'You and Magda have been living together for years.'

'Seven years,' I say.

'There now – you might as well be married! You have your escape routes I'll bet, your pressure release valves. We all need them.'

I shake my head and try to laugh.

'He's denying it, Kevin, but we know the truth, don't we? Oh yes sirree we do!'

Kevin slaps me on the back, a bit too hard I think. I can feel the imprint of his open hand on my right shoulder as we leave the prefab together and make our way to the pub.

'The night starts here,' Kevin says, as he wanders up to the bar to order the first round of drinks.

'So, you're not married, you and Magda?' Pete asks.

'No, it just never came up I suppose.'

'And what about kids? If you have a kid will you get married then?'

'Who knows.' I don't mention the pregnancy; I'm not sure why. I can see Kevin coming back from the bar with three pints on a tray and my stomach turns over with nerves and I realise I don't want to be here.

'We'll just have a couple,' I say quickly to Pete. 'I don't want you showing up drunk tomorrow for Amy.'

'Don't worry about that, Patrick. I'd be more worried about her on that score to be honest. Anyway, you'll get to meet Amy later on tonight.'

'She's coming along too?'

Pete looks at me and laughs. 'I don't suppose that's how they do things in Copenhagen but you're in Dublin now!' He laughs again. 'And worse than that, Patrick, you're in Swords. You know the drill – no one here gets out alive!'

At some point Pete must have gone home to change because now he is wearing a bright blue shirt and black jacket. I went out to a take-away during the evening and ate fish and chips on the street before going back inside to the party. I could have sneaked away, back to the hotel, but for some reason I didn't. I couldn't bear the thought of being on my own, even though no one is talking to me in the pub. Pete gives me the occasional grimace or smile as he chats to others and I nod hello to faces I haven't seen since school days, but most of the time I'm standing on my own in the middle of the group which gets bigger and bigger as the evening passes.

The noise level increases also and this helps as it ensures any conversations I do have are soon terminated. I accept all drinks given to me but do not finish them. Despite this I can feel myself getting drunk. I know I should have phoned Magda by now, but I don't want to betray my excessive behaviour and I know my voice would. Every now and again I look at my phone, fearing that she will call, so I finally text a brief message: *Out for drinks with Pete and the guys, call you in the morning, love P xx.*

Amy is much prettier in real life than in her photos. She is young looking and her smile almost disarms me. She hugs me without hesitation and tells me how much Pete has told her about me. I feel like a fraud, nodding and smiling back at her. She doesn't stay long and when she leaves I watch her for a while as she moves around the packed pub, pausing here and there to chat to friends. Once again, I'm not sure what I'm doing here. I never once told Magda about Pete over the years. The first she knew about him was when the wedding invitation arrived.

'How're you holding up there?' Kevin is beside me again. This time he brings a tray of shots and places one on the ledge in front of me.

'Get that down ya!'

I pick up the tiny glass and tip its contents down my throat and feel it burn. It is not a pleasant sensation, but for some reason Kevin seems to warm to me more because I have downed it.

'I see you met Amy then?'

'Yes, she's a really beautiful girl,' I say.

'Yeah, a stunner! Not sure how Pete managed it.' He laughs.

We are both looking across the room at Amy now, in awe of her, or in awe of Pete. She is talking to another girl, darker hair but not unlike her.

'That's her younger sister,' Kevin says, reading my mind. 'Alison. She looks a bit like Amy but that's where the similarities end. She's a bit up herself, if you know what I mean. She's a singer.'

'A singer?' I ask.

'Yeah, she plays guitar, writes her own songs and stuff. She seems to be doing well, has an album coming out soon I think. But she's what me Ma would have called a Consequence, you know?'

'Arrogant?' I ask.

'I dunno. Just thinks she's better than everyone else around here. One of those people who can't wait to get away from the place.'

I know he's having a go at me, but I choose to ignore it.

'Maybe she's just got ambition,' I say.

'Maybe,' Kevin says. He downs a shot quickly and moves off into the crowd with his tray.

After he leaves I can't take my eyes off Alison. She hasn't got the same beauty as her sister; her cheeks are rounded and when she smiles they dimple slightly. She is shorter, and her figure is hidden by her loose-fitting clothes: an oversized striped sweater over skinny black jeans and boots. When Amy leaves her she remains on her own on the far side of the room. No one comes near her as I watch. I am drawn to her, literally. I negotiate my way through the crowd towards her. She's drinking beer straight from the bottle; I note the brand and order her one on my way past the bar.

'Here you go,' I say, and I hand her the bottle.

'Yes! It's working at last – I knew it would someday!' She clenches her fist and pumps the air dramatically.

'Sorry?'

'I saw you, you know. I saw you looking at me and I thought to myself: this guy looks just the type to be susceptible…' She smiles, and those dimples appear in her moon face. Her eyes are big and round and brown; I can't help looking at them.

'Susceptible to what exactly?' I ask, playing along.

'You see?' she says, turning to address an invisible third party. 'I knew it the moment I clapped eyes on him.' She looks at me. 'You knew the meaning of the word "susceptible", so I know you're not from around here.'

'And that's a good thing?' I ask. It crosses my mind that perhaps this is flirting.

'God yeah, it's a good thing!'

Her smile fades, her eyes narrow.

'Hey, I know who you are now. You're Pete's mate from Denmark, aren't you?'

'Guilty,' I say. 'Patrick. But I have to admit I actually am from around here and I only live in Denmark.'

Her eyes widen again in mock fear.

'Yeah, but don't you see, you got away?' She pulls a goofy face. 'You was one of the lucky ones!'

'I did, I am, I suppose,' I say.

'So why are you back?' She tilts her head. Her question seems serious.

'For the wedding,' I say.

'No, really, why are you back? For Pete? You haven't seen him in years.'

'I know, but we were friends for years.'

She puts her hand on my upper arm and smiles. Those dimples appear.

'Don't look so worried. I'm just messing with you. I'm Alison, by the way.'

I can't help smiling back at her.

'So, what about you?' I say.

'What about me?'

'I hear you're a complete bitch.' I try to be deadly serious when I say it, but I can't suppress a smile.

'Ouch! Ow! That really hurts so much.' She laughs along with me. 'So, you've been talking to the locals I guess.'

'I hear you have ideas above your station,' I say.

'Well, I should hope so! You can understand where I'm coming from more than most I'd say. My guess is that while Pete obviously wants you here, most of the rest of them have no time for you.'

'We're like two peas then?' I say.

'Something like that.'

'But at least you have a recognisable talent – I'm just a nobody.'

'Ah, don't say that! I'm sure you have some skills. What do you work at?'

'Do we really have to do this?' I ask.

'Come on!'

'It's okay for you, you do something cool. Me? I'm just an engineer.'

'Okay, I can see why you didn't want to share that.' She laughs and enjoys the laugh a little too much.

'So tell me about the music career,' I say.

'Not much to tell. Lots of rehearsal, gigging, some radio, some recording – the usual stuff,' she says casually.

'Sounds great,' I say. 'I hear it's going well.'

'Don't believe all you hear.' She shakes her head and looks at me. She becomes serious again. 'I have a plan for the next few years and after that who knows… I might go back to college if it doesn't work out.'

I can feel my phone buzz in my pocket. I know it must be Magda.
'It's getting late,' I say. 'I think maybe I should go.'

'It's early,' she says. 'Stay. Look at the rest of them!' She
indicates the room; Pete and Amy are drinking and chatting
with different groups. 'The bride and groom aren't going
anywhere just yet.'

'No. I should go and get some sleep. I'm wrecked, I'm not used
to this level of drinking.'

'But you're coming tomorrow, to the wedding?'

'Yes, of course.'

'Come on then, I'll walk you down the road a bit. I want to have
a smoke anyway.'

We slip out as quickly as we can. Out on the street the town
looks desolate. Traffic is light and there are few people about. We
walk in the direction of my hotel, our arms brushing against each
other as we move. I feel like I'm living another life. For years I
walked these streets at night with my friends after the pub closed
or sometimes with a girl, looking for a quiet spot off the main
street where we could kiss or do more in some privacy.

We stop outside my hotel and I'm not sure what to do next. 'So,
I'll see you tomorrow,' I say.

'Until tomorrow then,' she says in her mock-serious tone.

I turn away, but she puts her hand on my sleeve and coughs.

'Ahem! You may kiss me now,' she says, pouting her lips,
closing her eyes.

I kiss her, and her lips are so soft. Her lips part and I let her
tongue in and it's warm and I feel myself getting aroused. I turn
and head for the door of the hotel without looking back.

'See ya tomorrow!' she calls.

It takes me ages before I can sleep. I look at the message from
Magda: *Sleep well love. Hope you're having a nice time. Love, M and
T x*. Then I lie awake scrolling through images of Alison I find on
social media pages belonging to my old friends. I feel isolated from
the world in this dingy room and don't want to think about anyone
or anything but her.

I sleep eventually but not for long enough. When the alarm sounds I feel lousy. I stand under the shower for ten minutes then stagger downstairs for breakfast. The smell of food in the dining room makes me want to retch, but I order anyhow, knowing I need to eat something ahead of the long day that stretches out before me. When it comes, all I can manage is some toast and three cups of tea. I feel lost. I wish I was at home with Magda. I go back up to the room and phone her, but it goes straight to her message. I don't know what to say so I hang up before the beep.

I get back into bed for a while and set an alarm, but again I can't sleep. I keep thinking of Magda and Alison, one after the other, as if I'm comparing them, looking for something they might have in common which I instinctively know does not exist.

The ceremony takes place in a large room in a country house hotel. The days of church weddings are passing in Ireland it seems. The room is decked out in ribbons and flowers and crowded with people. I search for Alison among the bridesmaids but can't find her. It is only when we move into the function room to have the meal that I notice her. She is sitting at a table near the back with a bunch of younger, bearded men and skinny elegant young women. She looks unlike herself, or unlike the version of herself I met last night. She wears a short black cocktail dress that shows a lot of cleavage, high heels, black tights. Her dark hair is piled on top of her head accentuating the roundness of her face and eyes. She sees me looking at her and raises a hand slowly in a nonchalant wave. I look away and take my seat at a table full of people I don't know who seem to know all about me.

The meal is torture and the speeches that follow seem endless. The only good news is that my hangover passes and the red wine makes me feel more relaxed than I actually am. When Pete mentions me in his speech, I realise I am slightly pissed, as I stand up and wish him and Amy all the very best. In the toilets I run into Kevin and he seems drunk already.

'You're a dark horse!' he says as he looks along the bank of urinals at me.

'Am I?' I ask.

'You stole off early last night,' he says, zipping himself up. 'You were seen. Nothing goes unseen in this town, Patrick. You should know that!'

He rinses his hands at the sink in a perfunctory way and shakes the excess water off onto the floor. I don't know what to say.

'I'm not sure what you mean,' I say, but whatever he says by way of reply is drowned by the roar of the hand dryer. All I know it that he is laughing as he leaves.

It's still early and I have no wish to go back to the dining room to make small talk with strangers, so I step outside into the hotel gardens. The sun is beginning to go down and the evening is mild. Looking back at the hotel with its chandelier-lit windows I appreciate for the first time what a beautiful location Pete and Amy have chosen for their wedding. My phone jumps into life. I know it's Magda, but I let it ring until it stops. Ahead of me a signpost points in the direction of a woodland walk, so I decide to take it. I walk for more than an hour without meeting a soul before I find my way back to the hotel.

Back in the function room I feel even more disconnected from everyone and everything around me. The music is too loud and everyone seems to be laughing or chattering or shouting to be heard above the noise. The bar is thronged but regardless I join the queue to get a drink. When I finally get to the bar I order a vodka and coke as well as a beer. I drink the vodka while I'm still at the bar before wandering off with the beer in my hand.

Alison is not where she was during the meal and I can't help feeling disappointed. I just want to talk to her again; to get past the awkwardness of the way I ran away from her last night.

The music stops at last and I look up to the stage and see Alison with a guitar in her hands. It suits her. She looks happy. She wants to play a song for her sister, she says, to wish her happiness on her wedding day. She starts to play and the whole room falls silent. Her voice is surprisingly powerful, the notes clear, but sometimes as she moves up and down the register her voice vibrates momentarily on the note. The first time it happens I think her voice has failed her when I hear the note waver, but I realise it's simply an idiosyncrasy in her voice, and I begin to wait impatiently for the next vibration to come. When she finishes the room erupts into applause and I notice how she blushes as she bows quickly and leaves the stage.

The DJ cranks it up again so I walk out to the foyer and sit down into a plush leather couch to get some peace.

'I was looking for you earlier. I was afraid you'd left.'

I look up at her. She looks anxious, not at all like the confident performer she was just moments before.

'Sit down,' I say. She sits beside me, perched on the edge of the cushion as if she might leave at any moment.

'You're much more popular than you imagine,' I say.

She smiles.

'Sometimes,' she says. 'But sometimes I don't want to be popular.'

I think I know what she means, but I don't say anything. I just look at her.

'You're not enjoying yourself?' she asks.

'No, I suppose not, but it doesn't matter,' I say. 'What about you? Your song was brilliant by the way; you have such a unique voice.'

'Stop, will you. You're making me blush.'

'No, really, you were very good.'

I want to place my hand on hers; it's all I can think about. And then I do. She doesn't take her hand away. Now we're sitting side by side, eyes front, with our hands joined on the couch between us.

'I know you have someone,' she says. 'It doesn't matter – well not to me. I just wanted to see you again, you know?' Still she doesn't look at me.

'I know,' I say. 'Me too.'

'It doesn't matter,' she says again.

'I'm not myself since I got here,' I say. 'Sorry, I'm not making excuses. I just feel lost somehow.' I want to look at her, but I won't let myself.

'We all do sometimes,' she says.

Neither of us say anything for a while. We can hear cheering and raucous singing coming from the function room across the foyer.

'I fly back tomorrow,' I say at last, and turn to look at her.

'I know,' she says, looking straight ahead.

I tell myself I don't know what I want, but deep, deep down I know I do. After a moment she gets up and walks towards the lifts. I follow her.

Printed in Great Britain
by Amazon

40401653R00026